CLARA, DARLING

CHACE VERITY

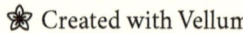

AUTHOR'S NOTE

Sadie's role on the radio show within *Clara, Darling* might be confusing for people who aren't familiar with the dizzy (or "Dumb Dora") type that was popular in the first half of the 20th century. Female comedians were often relegated to this character. The type was supposed to be laughed at because they didn't share the same logic as "normal" people. It was usually quite ableist, sexist, and racist. A lot of those jokes don't hold up well today.

There were exceptions, though. Gracie Allen of Burns & Allen is perhaps the most famous dizzy dame in American entertainment. She had a presence that made the audience root for her—and she had a partner who didn't mind letting her get the laughs at his expense. Her illogical logic was considered quite smart by audiences.

In *Clara, Darling*, Sadie resents the dizzy role, but that doesn't necessarily reflect the attitude all women in entertainment had about it back then. Some female comedians genuinely loved their dizzy characters, and I do not wish to erase their histories. Sadie's story is her own. I hope you enjoy it.

For content notes, please visit the story's page at chaceverity.com.

Best,

Chace "watching dry paint" Verity

CHAPTER ONE

DECEMBER 16, 1932

THE MOST IMPORTANT TASK IN PERFORMING RADIO shows was dressing well. Sadie Reynolds always spent the day before her husband's weekly radio show planning her outfit. She started with shoes, and then she worked her way up.

This week's outfit called for leather T-straps from Italy with decorative copper buckles. Beige silk stockings were a must, and they always had to be from Paris, just like the rest of her undergarments. A custom-tailored dark red frock flecked with bronze would be the centerpiece of her body, its sleeves above the elbows wide to make Sadie look powerful. Instead of wearing the complementary scarf around her neck, Sadie would tie it around her waist. A velvet capelet and matching gloves—also from Paris—would go well her copper monogrammed bag. To complete the outfit, a crushed velvet head wrap with a perky ribbon to make her look friendly.

Not that anyone would call Sadie Reynolds friendly, no matter how hard she tried. She always smiled in front of audiences and cameras, especially when she stood next to her husband of nine years. Sadie devoted her free time to planning the most ostentatious parties held in their palatial apartment on Fifth Avenue or their summer home in Vermont. Every person on the cold New York City streets who asked for help received at least one crisp dollar bill.

Alvin Reynolds earned money, and Sadie spent it—and everyone talked about her spending. Any time she stepped inside McCreery's, Best's, Ovington's, Bonwit Teller's, Saks, or Tiffany, everyone knew. Gossips in newspaper columns, "close friends" who thought Sadie wouldn't hear, Alvin... Oh, Alvin always talked about the damage Sadie did to his wallet.

Wasn't it a fair price to pay for what he did to her?

Sadie didn't hesitate to spray as much of her expensive Parisian perfume as she wanted, although she made sure it wouldn't be too much for the innocent studio audience. Alvin refused to work without an audience. He prided himself as a stage actor and a comedian. The truth was that he was a very insecure man, a fact Sadie had realized only after taking her vows to him.

Before she went to the studio, Sadie retouched her shimmering nails. She had gone to the salon earlier in the morning to get her dark brown hair coiffed properly, along with a manicure and pedicure. At least at the salon, everyone pretended they liked her.

During the lonely walk to the studio, with December's bitter air slashing her cheeks, Sadie longed for the warmth of Tennessee she had left behind long ago. It wasn't just the fact she spent money as fast as Alvin—or she, for Sadie also received a small pittance for her role on his radio show—earned it that made people wary of her. There was also the fact that she wasn't the right kind of rich person. Having come from Benton, Tennessee with no more than a sixth grade education under her belt and five dollars in her wallet, Sadie didn't have the same upbringing of New York's mightiest socialites.

The rich detested outsiders. There was a saying among them that in order to be a real New Yorker, one must have been born in New York or lived there for a full ten years. After twelve years of living in New York City, Sadie now understood that the rules never applied to anyone the elite didn't inherently like.

She was still an outsider, despite her tenure in

the city. Despite her knowing the most trustworthy bootleggers and the best place to get a ribeye steak. Despite being married to Alvin B. Reynolds, the comedic star of stage and radio who was from a well-to-do Long Island family.

Alvin's family had disapproved of him marrying a show girl, but he had done it anyway because he had claimed to be in love. Sadie hadn't been very sure of marriage to a man in the first place, but she had believed him. She had trusted his words, his heart.

Now, years later, Sadie understood that it was Alvin's prick doing all the talking, not his heart. The first time she discovered he had cheated on her, she had blamed herself for not being a better lover in bed. The second time, she vowed to learn everything about being a good wife in order to please Alvin and keep him home. The sixth or seventh time, Sadie figured out no amount of douching would prevent Alvin's faithlessness or the itch he had brought to her vagina. She moved into a different bedroom and refused to open her legs for him ever again.

Alvin had never stood up for his wife, but after that move, he began to participate in spreading rumors about her. How she only used him for money. How she hadn't been a virgin before they married (which was true, but he also hadn't been one). How she sometimes fainted after a radio show just to get attention. The hurtful words always got back to her in some form or fashion. Gossip was a cold that thrived in their social circle.

Everybody thought Sadie Reynolds was a gold digger, so why not play the part? She was three years away from turning forty and had no other options. It made it easier to pretend her life hadn't crumbled ever since the day her most darling—and only—friend had left.

Sadie swallowed hard before entering the radio station. It wouldn't do to cry here. Not before the show. She didn't have time to ruin her makeup. If she showed any weakness, she'd see her name everywhere in tomorrow's papers.

Besides. It would be Christmas soon. Christmas gave her a sense of normalcy. The holidays always rejuvenated her spirits and gave her the strength to get through the rest of the year.

She greeted the studio audience politely as she entered the stage with her script in her hands. She had about a dozen lines today. It wouldn't do if anyone upstaged Alvin on his own show, especially his wife. They didn't act like a married couple on the program. Instead, Sadie played his dizzy secretary, pitching her voice high so she could sound twenty years younger. There was never any romance between them. Alvin had his writers save their best flirts for episodes with glamorous female guest stars.

It was humiliating, but Sadie had stopped caring long ago. There was no one around her to tell her she could do better than him. Her own family, staunch Christians, had disowned her when she had announced her intentions to get into show business. Everybody involved in theater, movies, and radio were inherently immoral, according to the people whose last name she had once shared.

But Sadie hadn't gone to New York alone. Her best friend since childhood had also been seduced by the glitter and fame Broadway promised. Neither of them had wanted to settle down and have children. Not before they could see more of the world beyond the acres of farmland, ribbons of rivers, and a horizon sculpted with mountains.

The applause of an audience was louder than any river, and it used to be so much more refreshing. Sadie stared at her husband as the studio greeted him effusively. Alvin, with his peppery hair slicked to hide the bald spot that embarrassed him. Alvin, with his suit speckled with fresh flowers to trick people into believing he possessed a personality. Alvin, with his roving eyes, hoping to see if any woman in the first few rows wanted to bed him.

Once, Sadie used to examine the audience with those same eyes. If Alvin could have multiple women, why couldn't she? But none of the women ever had the qualities she wanted. Strong, dangerous eyes paired with a capricious smile. A formidable stance that could easily give way to a bout of silliness when the moment was right. Hair that looked like autumn in one light and spring in another.

There was only one woman Sadie could think of in the entire world that had everything she wanted, and that woman had been dead for nine years.

Sadie stared into the distance, right over the heads of the audience, as Alvin's show began. The orchestra opened with "Roaming for Romance."

As Alvin cut in with his jokes, spoken as if he had had anything to do with their clever syntax or punchiness, Sadie's attention veered to the glass booths off to the side. The station executives and sound control man in one, the sponsors in the other. There was another booth reserved for Alvin's special guests, but it was empty today.

Sadie's part soon arrived. Amidst a flurry of laughs, she approached the silver microphone. Her knuckles were nearly white from clenching the script.

Alvin set her up for her part by asking if Sadie had picked up his mail for him yet. The joke would be that she had picked up the mail from the "office" and then re-mailed it to his house. A classic dizzy Sadie blunder.

The real Sadie glanced at the empty booth again. This time, she caught a hint of spring in the empty room. Or was it autumn?

No, it was winter. The person's skin was far paler than Sadie's own white complexion. The stranger's thick brown hair glowed with bright silver streaks, and the wavy curls dangled loosely down her back. Her seemingly unkempt appearance stood out against the slim, shiny taffeta dress that had been popular ten years ago. Its color was hard to discern, but something about it was distinct. The kind of dress Clara had loved putting together with some fabric she'd buy off of stage costumers.

Clara.

Sadie stared harder, piecing together the vision before her.

"Secretary? Hello? Secretary? Where's my little secretary? She's supposed to be here right now."

Alvin stood right next to Sadie, yet his saccharine voice was distant. The world itself felt muted as the figure in the booth poked her head through the glass, giving the stunned actress a better look at her face.

The details were faint, but Sadie knew those brilliant eyes from anywhere. Clara Prescott—who had been dead since July 2, 1923—was gazing at her.

. . .

WITH ALL THIS INFORMATION, SADIE COULDN'T HELP but to faint.

CHAPTER TWO

DECEMBER 17, 1932

As soon as Sadie woke from her fainting spell, she made a dash for the door, desperate to find Clara. A few moments after tumbling out of bed, she realized she could feel the smooth carpet beneath her feet. She was back home, in her bedroom flush with earthy tones and paintings purchased directly from Greenwich Village artists. No nurses waited nearby. Alvin certainly wasn't anywhere near.

Daylight peered through her olive drapes. Sadie had been out for quite a while. No matter. She slipped out of yesterday's clothes and marched into her shoe closet. Black kitten heels were the first pair that caught her eye. After changing into a clean set of undergarments and silk stockings, Sadie put the rest of her outfit together. A black crepe dress with full sleeves and a short neckline that she could cover with a sky blue wool scarf adorned with silver buttons. Nothing too extravagant. A look that Clara would approve of.

"I don't know why you think shoes are the most important part of an outfit," Clara had once said. *"The dress is what men see first."*

"But I don't want men to look at my dresses. I want women to appreciate my outfit."

"Women look at dresses too."

"I don't. I want an excuse to look at their legs."

Except for Clara's dresses. Sadie always, always looked at her outfits. Clara had helped support her family by mending clothes as a child. Even after she started making better money in New York dancing in vaudeville shows, Clara's interest in dressmaking never waned. If anything, the big city opened her eyes to all new fabrics and styles.

When Clara went back to Tennessee, she vowed to open a dress shop, maybe in Nashville or Knoxville. Somewhere bigger than Benton, but not too overwhelming.

"New York's always been too big for me," Clara had confessed while packing up her apartment, the modest place on West 88th that she had once shared with Sadie.

Sadie opened a tube of dark red lipstick, thinking about how suddenly Clara had left. It had been a few months after Sadie married Alvin. The women had visited each other every day,

11

continuing their friendship like nothing had changed in their lives. They had been in the midst of trying out for grand parts on Broadway when Clara abruptly announced one morning she was going back to Benton.

Not once while they had lived together had Clara complained about the big city in any form or fashion. New York had been the place of dreams for both Sadie and Clara. The popular names written in lights, the tall buildings, the blending of culture and fashion, the excitement, the promise that working hard would get them riches one day —when did all of that become a burden to Clara?

As Sadie reapplied yesterday's makeup, her door swung open.

"I thought I heard you moving in here." Alvin leaned against the door frame, dressed only in his white underwear and socks. "What the hell happened last night?"

"I'm sorry." Sadie glanced at his reflection in the mirror briefly, and then she noted the way her brown eyes shook when she looked at him. Pathetic. She went back to focusing on her makeup. "I don't know what came over me. I must have worried you quite a bit."

"You fainted in the middle of a goddamn show! Everyone was worried about you!"

"I'm sorry." Sadie rose from her vanity and ambled to her collection of hats.

Alvin's glare could be felt across the room. "Where the hell do you think you're going at this hour? What about breakfast?"

"The station." She selected a velvet cap, also black in color. "Why don't you grab a meal with the Hubers? They always have an extra plate ready."

"The station? The show's already over. You fucked it up this week."

Sadie put on her cap without sparing him another look. She was used to his barbs. They hardly hurt her anymore. They stopped hurting after he rejected her first request for a divorce.

You can't survive without me.

That truth hurt more than anything else he had ever said. Sadie had no one. Better to live in luxury and be someone's property than to face the big world all alone.

"Fuck, you're so annoying," Alvin groaned. "The doctor said you need rest. Make sure you're well enough for next week. Harry already told the press you're fine, so don't make both me and my manager look like liars."

Alvin stormed off, leaving Sadie free to assess her outfit in her full length mirror. She wasn't the tidiest she could be, but it would do for now.

Sweat and yesterday's grime clung to her skin as she stepped outside. It was the same cutting temperature as the day before, but Sadie's body reacted differently today. For the first time in years, her heart drummed with hope.

Though she walked briskly, she stopped to give money to every person who asked. Sadie had her regulars who knew she was always good for at least a hot meal. Now was not the time to start disappointing them.

If anything, it was more important than ever to maintain her routine. No one looked at her differently when she handed them a dollar and held a brief conversation with them. No one treated her like a sick person. If anybody had heard about her fainting during last night's show, they weren't worried about her today.

Sadie entered the radio station, confident that nothing was wrong with her. This allowed the hope inside her to swell, swell to heights she hadn't seen since the day Clara and she had boarded the train to New York City.

That had been in 1921, around this time of the year. Sadie had planned on going to the big city alone after experiencing the way her family reacted to her dreams. The last thing Sadie wanted was to cause a rift between her best friend and her family. Sadie had decided get settled in New York alone and then do her best to convince Clara's family to give their blessing so their oldest daughter could pursue her dreams.

But when the day came for Sadie to leave, Clara

had met her at the train station. From a hundred feet away, Sadie had recognized her best friend by her brown velvet boots with the narrow heel. Clara's long, tawny hair had been tucked into place by a shimmering cream ribbon, reminiscent in color to her flowing dress with a wide lace collar. Her dark eyes had sparkled with a clear message. No protest could leave Sadie's lips when Clara had stolen her breath with her determination.

"We're going together."

The three most beautiful words that had ever been uttered.

The pain of losing her family hardly registered in Sadie's heart with Clara near. What good was dwelling on people who considered her a sinner for wanting to live her most authentic life? In the train, sharing a berth and soft touches, Sadie understood the woman next to her was her whole world.

It didn't hurt during that same trip that Clara and Sadie decided to get rid of their virginities. To each other, of course. Better to figure out how sex worked with a trusted friend than to be laughed at or hurt by someone else. Sadie had whispered her fears that first night, and Clara had echoed her. Already in close proximity with just their night garments on and no one in the berths above or across from them, the women explored each other thoroughly.

It had been a magnificent night. One they repeated a few times until they were sure they knew how to please other women.

When had they disclosed to each other that they favored women over men? Even now, Sadie didn't know. For as long as she had known Clara, she had known she liked women, and the reverse had been true for her friend. The idea of sleeping with men had never repulsed them, but it had seemed more like something that would have to happen, not an act of true desire. Just like getting married and, later, getting buried in the ground.

During their first year in New York, Sadie and Clara enjoyed sex with women, men, and people who were neither. Speakeasies had been good for both alcohol and sex. It was usually only the women the friends talked about long after the beds had gone cold. Clara had always wanted to know what Sadie's lovers had worn—and Sadie secretly had wanted to know if Clara's lovers had been better than her.

If only Sadie had realized then what her feelings had meant. She had only figured it out after it was far too late.

But now… Now that she was marching down the glossy halls of the radio station…

A few people stopped to talk with Sadie, but they all let her go when she curtly told them she had left something behind last night. Sadie carefully entered the studio and kept her eyes open. Nothing seemed out of the ordinary. A few people setting up for that evening's show. They attempted some greetings, but she waved them off while she crossed the carpeted stage.

The control booth was busy, as expected. She stopped in front of the booths for the sponsors and the special guests. Nobody was inside the sponsors' booth. Also expected.

The hope in her heart shriveled when she peered through the window into the last booth. The room was completely empty except for a table, a few chairs, some ashtrays, and a radio.

Sadie had already come this far, though, and she couldn't leave so soon. She opened the door and slipped inside the booth. Facing the door as she closed it, Sadie held her breath, hoping her wish would come true.

When she turned around, the room was no longer empty. The same marvelous sight Sadie had seen last night stared back at her.

The ethereal figure sat on top of the table, her legs swinging. No shoes. Just a pair of long feet, natural and beautiful, despite their partial opaqueness.

Sadie's gaze followed the legs past the taffeta dress, up to the intense face greeting her. Relief swept through Sadie when she met Clara's blazing eyes. They glowed brighter than the streaks in her hair. Even in death, Clara Prescott's beauty was one of a kind.

"Hello, darling," Sadie whispered.

Clara stopped swinging her legs. "You're not scared?"

Her voice was the same as it had been when she was alive. Not a note lower or stiffer. All the consonants were perfectly soft.

"Why would I be?" Sadie broke into a smile. "It's you."

After a pause, Clara returned her smile. Sadie could almost detect the nude lipstick Clara had always favored in life.

Then Clara disappeared.

Strangely, Sadie was happier than ever.

CHAPTER THREE

DECEMBER 23, 1932

SADIE FELT LIKE SHE HAD TWO LIVES FOR THE NEXT few days. In one life, she was Sadie Reynolds, the wife of Alvin B. Reynolds, the gold digger of Fifth Avenue, the former chorus show girl who now danced with demeaning lines on radio. In her other life, she was Sadie, the woman who had finally been reunited with her best friend.

Every day, Sadie went to the radio station and visited with Clara. Clara didn't usually stay for long, and she never left the glass booth. Their conversations were limited. Sadie described her outfit each day, explaining what was in style and where each piece had come from. Clara usually said nothing, but her bright gaze followed the flow of Sadie's words. Sometimes, Sadie consulted with Clara about what presents to buy for Alvin's family that Christmas.

Difficult questions pressed at Sadie's heart, yes, but she knew now wasn't the time to approach them. The staff and stars at the radio station could easily see through the glass booth. Clara's attention often veered to the window when it got too busy, and she became as translucent as glass right before disappearing. The heavier conversations would need to be saved for when they were truly alone.

Besides, Sadie didn't *need* those questions answered. Clara had brought the warm winds of Tennessee with her, gifting New York with unseasonably pleasant weather. That was a gift almost as good as the ghost herself. Warmth and good company—what else could a woman want?

Soon, it was Friday again. Time for another show.

Sadie showed up at the radio station early to visit with Clara before rehearsal. That afternoon, though, with the stage full of everyone needed for the program, there was no sign of her darling friend. This caused a fracture in her heart. It would have been nice to be Sadie for a while before she had to turn into Mrs. Alvin B. Reynolds or the nameless secretary.

Alvin was in quite a mood during rehearsal. He didn't like the orchestra's version of "Silent Night." The sponsors didn't like some of the jokes about their product in the script. The show was two minutes too long, and the show's writers weren't sure where to trim.

"Let's start again from the part where the secretary comes in." Alvin gestured to his wife, but he didn't spare her a single look. "Try to speak faster, okay? If you don't dawdle during your part, we can get another few seconds. Remember, we're in the city, not the farm."

She shot him a glare, but she didn't argue with him. He was the boss.

Alvin signaled to the control booth, where the writers and technician were huddled. "Bob, start tracking time once I introduce Sadie."

Everyone went quiet. Bob held his pocket watch with his palm raised, indicating he was ready.

Alvin spoke into the microphone first. "Say, that's a pretty good joke. I should write that down. Secretary, where are you?"

"I'm here!" Sadie's throat burned as she pitched her voice high, turning into the dizzy secretary that existed solely to make Alvin look competent. "What can I do for you, Mr. Reynolds?"

"Write this down for me. 'What's more boring than watching paint dry?'"

Sadie faked a giggle. "Oh, I don't know, Mr. Reynolds! What's more boring than watching paint dry?"

"No, no, I want you to—" Alvin groaned. "What the hell's going on, Bob?"

The door to the control booth swung open. Bob poked his head out. "My, uh, watch isn't working. It just suddenly stopped."

"You didn't wind it up?" A snarl, tinted with superiority, slipped from Alvin's lips. "Isn't there a clock in there?"

"Yeah, but the room's clock is also broken," Bob answered.

Alvin rolled his eyes and removed his golden watch from his coat's pocket. "Here. Use mine."

Bob grabbed it from him and gave it a quick glimpse. "Er, this is also no good."

While everyone on set checked their watches, Sadie's eyes darted to Clara's booth. No sign of her long, free hair or the brilliance emanating from her eyes. Still, she was somewhere near. She had to be.

Time started moving forward again after someone grabbed a clock from a different set. Everyone took their places again.

"All right, let's try this again." Alvin made no attempt to give anyone a friendly or reassuring face. Sweat dripped down the back of his neck. Sadie made a mental note to pick up a clean shirt for him when she went back home between rehearsal and the live show. "From the secretary's entrance!"

Bob raised his palm.

Alvin laughed to himself. "Say, that's a pretty good joke. I should write that down. Secretary, where are you?"

"I'm here!" Sadie's throat roared with fire. Usually, it wasn't this difficult to play the part. "What can I do for you, Mr. Reynolds?"

"Write this down for me. 'What's more boring than watching paint dry?'"

Before Sadie could force one of those goofy giggles out of her, the lights went out.

"Oh, hell!" Alvin groaned. "Does this station not pay the goddamn light bill?"

Alvin and the staff scuffled about with only a match's fire to guide them in the darkness, trying to figure out what happened.

Sadie's guide, however, was Clara. Clara sat in the middle of the front row. Her glowing eyes revealed the frown stitched on her face. Sadie rolled up her script and joined Clara off the stage. No one noticed when she moved.

"Is all of this your doing, darling?" Sadie asked in a low voice.

Clara nodded, glaring at the stage.

Sadie held back her laughter and took the seat next to her. "Delightful. Why have you decided to tamper with our rehearsal?"

"You're too smart for this role."

"The secretary role?" Sadie glanced at the stage.

A few lit cigarettes broke the tedium of the darkness. The noise was busy, too busy for her ears to catch any specific conversation. "It's just a part. Alvin decided that was the best part I could play on his show. What else can I do?"

Clara's glare remained focus on the set. "Alvin's wrong."

"Is he?" Sadie crushed the rolled up script in her hands. "Better than dancing until my ankles get twisted for fifteen or twenty dollars a week, isn't it?"

"This isn't what you wanted."

Sadie had no immediate response. Clara spoke the truth. But it'd be too humiliating to admit that much to her best friend. Clara had been her champion in life. Wouldn't it upset Clara to hear that this whole time she had been dead, Sadie had withered into a ghost of her former self?

Suddenly, Clara turned to Sadie. Right there, with their audience in the dark, Clara brought her hand to Sadie's cheek. Sadie stayed still, relishing the cold shiver that shot down her back. It wasn't the same as it had been with their bare skins cocooning under a blanket together, but the sensation was comforting.

Clara leaned in and pressed a kiss to Sadie's lips. Light, quick, a tease that couldn't quite be felt. A kiss all the same.

"I shouldn't have…" Clara mumbled into Sadie's mouth.

"Shouldn't have what?" Sadie whispered. She wasn't ready to have this conversation here, but so much of her life had already been pulled from her control. Better to go with the flow than to continue living in doubt. "Kissed me? Gone back to Benton?"

Instead of finishing her sentence, Clara vanished. Once the coolness of her touch evaporated, the lights turned back on.

"Jesus. About time." Alvin checked his watch and let out a long, puerile groan. "Places, everyone! We're going to finish this goddamn rehearsal, or I'll—"

While he ranted, everyone took their places. Everyone but Sadie. She continued sitting in her chair, not quite ready to be Mrs. Reynolds or the secretary or anyone at all.

Alvin caught her in her daze. The snarl he threw in her direction was distasteful. It hardly woke her from her thoughts.

"Woman, did you not hear me?" Alvin asked. "Get up here."

Sadie met his wide-eyed glare and wondered why she ever married him in the first place. How had she been so easily charmed by his words and his gifts?

"Alvin asked me to marry him." She remembered telling Clara after coming home one night,

sporting a new pair of diamond earrings. *"He says I won't wear cheap jewelry or be in gaudy productions anymore if I marry him."*

Clara had said nothing at first. She had instead helped Sadie out of her dress. Her broad hands had then caressed Sadie's bare shoulders. Had Sadie moaned then? She couldn't remember. She only remembered liking the way Clara touched her, which had made Alvin's proposal even more confusing. It had been several months since the roommates had last been intimate with each other.

"I don't love him. Not like the way a wife should love her husband. He's good for a tumble and some fun, but do I want to spend my life with him?"

"You could be safe," Clara had finally said. *"A man has to protect his wife. Do you think Alvin would keep you safe?"*

"Safe from what?"

"People who don't appreciate you as you are."

Sadie couldn't remember quite how the rest of the conversation had gone. Just that Clara had ultimately given her blessing for their marriage.

Was Clara back because of Alvin? Sadie's heart raced with possibilities of what her return could truly mean.

"Sadie!" Alvin screamed. "Get the fuck up here!"

She didn't want to. She refused, even. There had to be a way to avoid it.

Perhaps she could make her own way.

Sadie carefully formed her next sentence. "The show's too long. Cut my part this week. It's not funny, anyway."

Alvin gaped at her. "Excuse me? Who are you to tell me what's funny or not funny? Are you in the writers' room with me and the guys? No, you're not."

Bob cleared his throat. "Actually, I was just thinking we should cut that scene."

Alvin turned his attention to him. "But *I* wrote this scene."

Bob rubbed the back of his neck.

Sadie rose to her feet and left her script in the chair, no longer needing it.

In fact, she wondered if she would ever need a script again.

CHAPTER FOUR

DECEMBER 24, 1932

"You're quitting the show?"

"Yes."

Sadie served Alvin his breakfast. Steak and eggs. As usual, he was only wearing his underwear and hadn't bothered to wash his face or shave yet.

She took a seat across from him at the table, helping herself to a large grapefruit and a glass of milk. She would eat a bigger lunch while she was out finishing her Christmas shopping.

Alvin began cutting his steak into pieces. "Did you forget you've got a contract?"

"I didn't." Sadie sipped her milk. "I want out. I don't want to do the show anymore."

"Well, you're not quitting the show. Not until I say you can quit."

Sadie sighed. "I figured you would say as much."

Alvin crammed a huge slice of steak into his mouth and talked with his mouth full. "You wanna make me look like a pansy who can't keep his wife on his own damn show?"

"No, of course not." Sadie poked at her grapefruit with her spoon. "But I don't think my part suits me."

"Why the hell not? You've got no brains up there." Alvin shoved the rest of the steak in his mouth and rose from his chair, leaving the eggs behind. "Stop trying to cause a fuss. It's Christmas."

Sadie's gaze followed him as he circled the dining table. "Speaking of Christmas, what time are your parents expecting us tomorrow? I should be able to finish all of my shopping today, but I want to be sure I have everything wrapped in time."

"We're not going there this year." Alvin swallowed what was left in his mouth. "I've got a business trip to New Jersey to make tonight. Gotta stay until Monday."

"Business? During the holidays?" Sadie arched an eyebrow.

"He's Jewish."

"It's Chanukah this week."

Alvin picked up Sadie's milk and finished the glass off for himself. "What did you buy my mother? Is it under the tree?"

Sadie's voice tightened as he set the empty glass

before her. "A lovely perfume and cold cream set from Paris."

"Get another set. I'm going to take this one with me."

"For your business meeting?" Sadie stared blankly at him. "With a man?"

"Yeah, he's got a wife. Have my family's gifts delivered tomorrow morning, all right? Make sure there's an extra big box of Cuban cigars for my father. I'll call my folks and explain everything. Say you're sick or something."

Sadie watched Alvin leave the dining room. There was no business meeting. She knew that.

It infuriated her that she wasn't even mad about him leaving her alone during the holidays to be with another woman. She also wasn't angry that she had inadvertently bought her husband's lover a present and wrapped it beautifully for her. It hardly registered with her that she was also being used by Alvin so he could skip his other familial obligations to get his dick wet.

She was furious at herself for putting up with all of this. She hadn't even managed to quit the show like she wanted. Clara would be so disappointed in her.

Clara.

Where would she be at for Christmas?

Sadie wandered into the living room, where a fresh green fir tree had been delivered earlier in the week. She hadn't decorated yet. Usually, Alvin and she decorated it together. Even though their marriage hadn't been a happy one for some time, they at least found some joy playing music and having drinks on Christmas Eve before going out to a big party together.

Now there wouldn't be anyone here tonight but Sadie. And tomorrow, there wouldn't be any turkey, gravy, mashed potatoes, French peas, creamed onions, cranberry sauce, or pudding. Just another grapefruit and glass of milk, perhaps. Lots of silence. What a dreadful holiday.

Sadie hardly put any thought into her outfit as she got ready for the day. Some heels that didn't hurt her arches too much, a dress that didn't call attention to her, a coat light enough for the warm day, a hat wide enough to mask her face. Just enough clothes to blend in with the crowds of New York.

She did her shopping dutifully. Arranged for everything to be delivered promptly at eight o'clock the next morning to the in-laws who wouldn't be missing her. She paid for someone else to wrap the remaining gifts, no longer in the mood to do it herself.

After a brisk lunch at a diner consisting of some vegetable soup and a wedge of bread, Sadie returned to the house. She had to deliver some gifts to the radio station. The station would be open in the morning, but she preferred going now. Anything to keep busy.

As usual, Sadie stopped to give anyone who asked for money a dollar or two. Today, though, she didn't have the patience for small talk. She had to keep moving. Any words of gratitude people gave her never reached her ears.

She left the bundle of gifts with the radio station's head secretary. Normally, Sadie and Alvin would go around together to be sure each executive and staff member received their gift. But nothing about today was normal, was it?

Maybe that's why she was unnerved. It was the holidays. It should have been a normal holiday. That was part of what Alvin had promised when he married her. To keep her company for all her days.

Sadie stood in the hallway, close to the door leading to the set where Clara resided. Her heart swelled as she rested her hand on the doorknob. Mad as she was at herself and her situation, she still wanted to see Clara.

No one was on the set when Sadie entered. The lights were dim. Not even an usher or janitor could be seen getting ready for that evening's program. Somehow, this also irritated her.

She crossed the stage, headed for the glass booth. But Clara met Sadie halfway. The two friends convened at the silver microphone, the device that channeled a single thought into thousands of homes.

Clara greeted Sadie by wrapping her cold arms around Sadie's warm body.

Sadie forgot all her raw anger at once. Why was she so mad about not having a normal Christmas? She didn't want Alvin. She didn't want to dine with his family who looked down on her. She didn't want to pretend she was someone other than herself.

Sadie ran her fingers through the translucent tendrils of Clara's hair. Each stroke sent a wave of pleasure through Sadie. There wasn't much she could truly grab as it was like caressing the wind, but the feelings stirred inside her were real.

"Hello, darling," Sadie murmured. "What are you doing for Christmas?"

"Christmas?"

"It's tomorrow." Sadie peered into Clara's eyes. Their radiance had softened, as if her own guard was down. "You're going to be here, aren't you?"

The silence that ensued answered the question clearly.

"Come home with me." Sadie uselessly looked for a place to rest her hands. "You can leave here, can't you? You got here somehow. You weren't here when you...when you..."

Clara finished her sentence. "When I died."

"When you died," Sadie echoed softly.

33

She watched her friend float around the small stage. It was a dance, but it also wasn't. Clara's bare feet never touched the floor while she paced in her own way.

Had Clara not been wearing shoes when she died?

According to her obituary, Clara had passed following a brief illness. Influenza or pneumonia, probably. Whatever it was, Sadie had been beside herself, certain that Clara would have survived her illness if she had never left. In New York City, Clara would have had quick access to the best medical care, and Sadie would have paid for every cent. She also would have been her nurse, seeing that Clara was taken care of every minute of every day.

Sadie had tried to get more information from Clara's family, but Clara's mother had only written Sadie about her daughter's passing a month after the funeral. She had also requested in that first, and only, letter that Sadie say her goodbyes in a New York church instead of returning to Tennessee.

But what good was a church some seven or eight hundred miles away? Sadie tried, but she hadn't been able to say goodbye at all.

"You can leave, can't you?" Sadie asked.

Clara stopped in front of Sadie. "You want me to come with you?"

Sadie broke into a smile. "You can, can't you? Come with me! It'll be just you and me. No Alvin. No Santa Claus. Just you and me."

"Where's Alvin?"

Sadie kept her smile, despite her heart wavering. "Fucking some poor woman in New Jersey. He won't bother us. Just follow me, okay?"

"Do you know what you're asking?"

"I do!" Sadie tried to grasp her friend's hand, but she only felt a cool breeze wrap around her own hands. "It'll be like the old days."

"And then what?"

The brightness returned to Clara's eyes. Something about the glow was dangerous. Thrilling, but dangerous. As if they were a window to a realm that would free Sadie from her current existence.

She wanted to go with Clara, no matter what, but did she have any right to be with her? Really be with her?

"What do you mean?" Sadie averted her gaze as she asked the question. "What do you want me to say?"

"Why won't you ask why I'm *here*?" Clara brought her fingers to Sadie's chin. "Why won't you ask how I heard your voice on the radio from beyond the grave? How I heard only a shadow of the vividness you used to possess? How I fought the way life and death works to come back?"

Sadie kept her attention on the carpeted floor. She deserved this scolding, but she didn't enjoy it.

Something shifted in Clara's voice as she continued speaking. A crackle, like a radio tuning into almost the right frequency.

"Why won't you ask me why I left you? Why won't you blame me for leaving you alone with Alvin? I should have never told you to marry him."

Guilt. Clara was here because she was laced in *guilt*.

Sadie shifted her head to look at Clara again, but her friend had already disappeared.

For a long time, Sadie stood alone with only a few dim lights to keep her from total darkness. There was a lot to digest. It made sense why Clara had spoken relatively little since returning.

But why did she carry so much guilt about Alvin? Did Clara think Sadie resented her? Didn't she know there was nothing that Clara Prescott could ever do to make Sadie think less of her?

Once she felt brave, Sadie whispered her address into the microphone. She followed it up with a promise.

"I won't hide from anything."

CHAPTER FIVE

DECEMBER 24, 1932

WHEN SADIE CAME HOME, SHE MET WITH A DELIVERY man who had come to pick up her in-laws' Christmas gifts. She tipped him ten dollars as he left. The only presents under the tree now were Alvin's. Ties from Paris, a golden waist coat from Italy, shirts made from Chinese silk, a variety of candy from multiple sweet shops in Chicago and Philadelphia, socks and long underwear from England. Each gift had been beautifully wrapped with, well, not love. Hope, maybe.

Her interaction with Clara clouded her thoughts as she took a bath. She couldn't understand why Clara was riddled with guilt. None of this had been her fault. Even though Clara had designed her wedding dress, a long velvet dress with a white capelet to keep her shoulders warm, Sadie had still chosen to take her vows at the courthouse.

Sadie didn't bother with makeup or underwear after getting out of the bath. She selected a pair of silk slippers and paired them with a fairly simple cream negligee, its only flourish being the ruching on the wide sleeves.

Though it was warm outside, Sadie decided to start a fire in the fireplace. It kept her company while she trimmed the Christmas tree with silver tinsel, beads that looked like pearls, and a few spherical ornaments. With the help of a dining chair, she managed to place the delicately crafted angel on top.

Sadie then opened one of Alvin's gifts—an assortment of chocolate filled with sweet creams—and tossed the paper and ribbon into the fire. She opened a bottle of wine, a gift from one of her bootlegger contacts, and made herself comfortable on the fur rug in front of the fire.

She watched the fire and slowly consumed her treats. Night flooded through the windows. Her thoughts swam with Clara. Their past. Their tenuous present. Their unknown future.

"I can't eat just sweets," Clara had said during their first Christmas in New York. They had landed a cheap flat furnished with the bare necessities. No kitchen. A shared bathroom down

the hallway. Only a few rats and bugs, nothing scary for two farm girls. *"I need something salty too."*

She then had placed a small burlap bag of mixed nuts next to the bags of licorice and gumdrops Sadie had purchased. Their Christmas feast with what few pennies they had left after securing shelter.

It had been a perfect Christmas. Two close friends starting to live their dreams. Together.

Sadie rose from the rug and meandered into the kitchen. After checking the cabinets, she found a bag of peanuts and placed them in a crystal bowl, cracking the shell off each one so their hidden gold could be readily eaten. It was possible Clara didn't need to eat now, but it would be rude to invite her over and not have something palatable to her available.

When Sadie returned to the living room, she was delighted to see she was no longer alone. Clara inspected the Christmas tree with an open curiosity. By the fire's orange glow, she looked so soft and warm. The fire might have very well danced into her bright eyes.

"Hello, darling." Sadie crossed the room and took her seat on the rug. She set the bowl of peanuts next to her half-eaten box of chocolates and mostly consumed wine. "Do you like the tree?"

Clara sat next to Sadie at once. She didn't

transition from standing to sitting like the living. She simply appeared in that position.

Sadie relished the fire's heat on one side of her and the coolness of Clara on the other. "Was it hard to find this place?"

Clara's gaze swept over the snacks. Her silence was colder than her ethereal form.

Thinking back to her earlier promise, Sadie finished the rest of her wine. "Did you come back because you feel guilty?"

There was no hesitation in her friend's response. "Yes."

"What about?" Sadie set her empty bottle by the fire and grabbed a single peanut. "I'm doing all right, don't you think?"

"Don't lie."

Even when she had been alive, Clara had had a gift for winding the truth out of Sadie. They had grown up together. They had gone through their first bleeds together, quit school together when their families needed them more, discovered Cecil B. Demille's craft together during trips to Chattanooga before the Great Influenza epidemic closed the theaters. Every nuance to one's voice could never be lost on the other.

"All right, so I'm not happy." Sadie tossed the peanut into the fire. "But I have a job in radio, nice shoes, three meals a day, and a warm bed to sleep in every night."

"Alvin was supposed to keep you safe."

Sadie stuffed her mouth with a chocolate and spoke while she chewed. "Aren't I safe? My feet are softer than they've ever been, Alvin doesn't beat me, and that itch he brought to my pussy hasn't come back in a while."

"That bastard."

"Yeah, I guess that wasn't safe of him." Sadie let a sigh escape her. She longed for a smoke, but she had left her cigarettes in her purse, hanging up on its hook in her bedroom. All the way down the hall. Too far away from Clara. "Maybe I'm not doing too great, but it's not your fault. At all."

"Yes, it is. I shouldn't have left."

"But you said you hated the big city." Sadie paused after those words left her. It also felt like her heart had paused with her. The doubt that had been in her brain for so long grew into an answer. "You lied to me about that, didn't you?"

"I'm sorry."

Clara's presence seemed small during that apology. Clara had always been taller than Sadie. She had always been the light of every room she occupied. She had always effortlessly stole Sadie's attention no matter where they were.

"Why?" Sadie tried to hide her nerves by eating another piece of chocolate. Somehow, she sensed she wouldn't like the answer to her next question. "Why'd you really leave?"

"Alvin said I needed to leave."

Sadie miraculously managed not to choke on her candy. It landed in her stomach like coal. "Alvin?"

Alvin had never mentioned having anything to do with Clara leaving. In fact, he had been quite sweet to Sadie during the first days following Clara's departure. He had promised they could have Clara visit them every Christmas, and if she wouldn't come back to New York, then they would go to Tennessee to visit her. Any time Sadie wanted, they would go. And then when Clara died, he had arranged for flowers to be sent to Clara's grave monthly.

Hadn't he?

"He said when we were together, it was obvious you'd rather have a wife than a husband." Clara stayed by Sadie's side, but she cast her attention away from the fire, away from Sadie, away from the Christmas tree, away from anything that might bring joy. "He said the best way to keep you safe was for me to get out of town. Then he would make sure everyone around you thought you were, well, someone you're not."

"Wait." Sadie tried to get Clara to face her, but her hands went through her friend's body. "You left for me?"

Clara nodded.

Oh.

"That's why you came back," Sadie said in a low voice. "Alvin didn't keep his end of the bargain."

Clara said nothing.

"Is there something more?" Sadie asked. "Tell me."

To Sadie's delight, Clara turned to her again. It was nice to see the details of her face—the slope of her nose, the dimple in her chin, the cupid's bow of a mouth that looked like it needed a kiss. No matter how uncomfortable of a conversation they were having, Sadie was so damned happy she was having it with Clara.

"Tell me everything," Sadie implored. "Please."

"I should have never left you." Anger scratched Clara's voice, like a radio signal gaining strength. "I should have stayed here after Alvin told me to leave. I should have told you I love you. I should have fucked you until *everyone* knew you were *my* wife. I should have showered you with all the love you deserve instead of hoping someone more approved by this stifled society would suffice. You're perfect the way you are."

The fire jumped to Sadie's heart and set it racing. Her heart pumped enough blood into her brain to make everything clear to Sadie. Clara hadn't come back to scold Sadie or clear up her own guilt.

Clara Prescott had come back from the grave to confess her love.

Time and time again, Clara proved she would always be there for Sadie. This time, Sadie wanted —needed—to demonstrate her own affections. No matter what it took, she was ready to prove she'd also always be there for Clara. It didn't matter what anyone else in the world thought. No one mattered but Clara.

"Then don't leave me ever again," Sadie quietly said. "I love you too much to watch you leave again. I'll follow you, if I must."

"Did you think I was going to leave you again?"

The question didn't come out like a threat, though Clara asked it sharply. Instead, her growing glare shot a thrill through Sadie. It was a lick of something she hadn't felt in so long. She leaned back, supported by her elbows, and allowed Clara to do what she wished.

"I'm not leaving you ever again," Clara stated, climbing on top of Sadie.

She hovered over the other woman, their faces close, reminiscent to that first night on the train to New York together. The first two climaxes between them had occurred side by side. The third had been in a position just like this, except their mouths had been inseparable. Clara had quickly figured out how to rub Sadie just right in any position.

Could Sadie still pull off multiple climaxes in a single night like she had in her twenties? When she self-pleasured these days, it was a one time peak. No beautiful woman next to her to motivate her for another. No desire to work for a relief she didn't need.

"Take me," Sadie said softly, dying to find out the answer to her question. "I want you, darling. I don't want anyone but you."

"No one else?"

A gush of cold rippled through Sadie. The sash to her negligee had become untied. She wriggled her hips, allowing more of her body to be unwrapped like a present. In this state of undress, Sadie found it easier to unwrap her heart.

"If there's anything about the past I wish I could change, I wish that I had understood how much I loved you back then. Then I would have never married Alvin. I would have never married any man. I would have lived with you and only you."

Clara remained still. Then, a slight curve of her lips gave way to a soft smile. That wonderful expression soothed all the wounds Sadie's soul had accumulated over the past several years.

"Take me," Sadie repeated, spreading her legs. "I missed you so much."

Ice drew to her lips, a kiss from her darling Clara. The chill didn't bother Sadie since they had the fire roaring next to them. Even if it were uncomfortable, she doubted she could stop herself from grasping at Clara's inviting lips. Sex with Clara had been a transcendent experience in the past—what would it be like now?

The chill spread from Sadie's mouth to her nipples, causing her to shiver. Somehow, Clara was kissing both her lips and her breasts. Sadie could only return Clara's affections with her mouth. Once Sadie moved her arms to lie flat on her back and free her fingers for adventure, a gentle pressure kept her arms in place.

"I missed you more." Clara's confession came out like a possessive growl. Her eyes glowed so fiercely, Sadie had to keep her eyes closed. "I'm claiming you first."

Sadie relaxed her body and let Clara have her way. "Take me, darling."

The same thrilling sensations delighting Sadie's mouth and breasts teased her stomach. Clara stopped at her navel, giving a touch that sent electricity through Sadie. Oh, she had forgotten how much Clara knew what her body liked. A current glided across Sadie's hips and thighs, pushing Sadie's legs to open wider.

Oh, Clara was kissing her in her most intimate area. While still giving her lips and her nipples an equal amount of attention, Clara flooded Sadie with pleasure. Sadie had been so tightly wound up for years, she quickly started rocking with Clara's ministrations. Touches were stolen everywhere as

Sadie moved, prying many needy moans from her trembling lips.

"You're mine now," Clara murmured. "I won't let anyone else have you."

In that frenzied mix of charged emotions and escalating sensations, a plea surged through Sadie's mind. She couldn't keep it inside her.

"Take me, darling," Sadie gasped. "I'm yours. Take me. Take me away from here."

From Alvin. From the radio. From the gossips. From New York, the place where her dreams had long since shattered. From the misery of living as someone she wasn't.

Clara could feel all those unspoken words by now, Sadie could tell. The cold and the indescribable pleasure that followed it had penetrated her. Clara claimed her with currents that thrusted into every hole Sadie wanted her in— and Sadie was quite greedy—filling Sadie until she couldn't take it anymore.

She came once, and she came loudly, and Clara gave her a moment to gather her senses—then she started over. They danced the same movements on that soft rug over and over. They repeated their vows, increasing the intensity of their passion with each encore, until Sadie had thoroughly soaked through her negligee and the rug itself.

She had enjoyed six climaxes over the past hour. Now, the lust in her brain had her curious about other ways they could explore their new relationship.

"How do I pleasure you?" she asked, opening her eyes. "I want to touch you too."

Clara studied her carefully. "Let me in."

A request that Sadie didn't fully understand, but she trusted Clara. There was no need to keep anything from her love. Sadie relaxed as much as she could.

Then, she noticed Clara had disappeared. But she was warm inside. Very warm. So warm that she felt the need to touch her body. Visions of Clara's toned calves and quivering thighs came to Sadie's mind. She remembered so many details of Clara's body as she touched herself. The notes of approval that came out of Sadie's mouth weren't hers. Those lovely sounds belonged to Clara.

Darling, do you like this? Sadie thought, unable to speak for herself.

"Yes," Clara answered through her.

Show me where you want me to touch you.

Momentarily, Sadie lost control of her body. Being possessed wasn't as scary as books and movies had made it seem. It was thrilling, watching her hand journey to the slickness between her legs.

"Here," Clara said softly. "It's been so long. Help me, Sadie."

Of course, darling.

Sadie palmed her clit, stuck two fingers inside her, and gave Clara just what she wanted. She worked fast, not wishing to deny her love some much needed relief. She could not only hear Clara's gratitude, but she could also feel it. Every ripple of pleasure echoed through her body.

Clara climaxed in a burst of short, breathy groans. She sounded divine. She felt divine. Everything about Clara was divine.

Shortly after Clara, Sadie found herself at her peak again.

After that roll of bliss, Sadie briefly became overwhelmed with fury. They could have been experiencing such joy together all this time. If only Alvin hadn't—

"Don't think about him," Clara interrupted. "Tonight, it's us."

She was right. Alvin would be dealt with later.

Sadie made sure to give Clara—and herself— enough pleasure that night to make up for lost time.

CHAPTER SIX

DECEMBER 26, 1932

SADIE AND CLARA ENJOYED ALL OF CHRISTMAS together. Sadie woke up late in the afternoon after their long night of passion. Joy brimmed within her when she found Clara stretched out on the bed next to her.

The pair spent the day in the living room, exchanging stories and slowly burning all of Alvin's Christmas presents—except the candy—in the fire. Sadie found a diner that was willing to deliver her a hot meal of sliced turkey with all the trimmings and sides she dreamed of. It was a perfect holiday.

They repeated their lovemaking through Monday morning, sometimes in different parts of the house. Whenever a single wisp of desire left Sadie's lips, the two became entangled with each other. They were both so eager, and it was wonderful to feel wanted.

While sharing one body in the bath, they came up with a plan to get everything they wanted. Sadie would ask Alvin for a divorce when he came back later. She'd also quit the show. She wouldn't take no for an answer for either demand. If he wanted all her jewelry and clothes, he could have them. He could say whatever he wanted about her to the newspapers and to the people who weren't her friends. Before the New Year rolled around, Sadie would be living away from him and starting her life again.

Clara left Sadie's body when Alvin came back. By now, Sadie was dressed and ready to rush to any lawyer's office that might be open that day. She had chosen a pair of black lace up ankle boots to start her outfit. There wasn't a need to dress heavy since it was still warm outside. A hand-knitted blouse with red and white horizontal stripes made her look flashy, as did the red tweed skirt she had chosen. Her lipstick matched her skirt better than it did the blouse. She accessorized lightly, choosing only a black belt to wrap around her waist. To finish her outfit, she selected a pair of white cashmere gloves and a small black velvet hat.

Sadie wasn't sure where Clara had gone, but she knew she couldn't be far. Still, when Sadie heard the front door open, she wished she could feel the currents of Clara's presence.

"I'm home!"

Alvin's voice rang through the apartment, full of saccharine cheer. Sadie grabbed her purse and marched down the hallway. She momentarily stopped halfway when she noticed the bundle of wrapped presents in his arms.

"Come here, woman, I got you some gifts." Alvin kicked off his shoes and waltzed into the living room. "You didn't think I forgot you, did you?"

Sadie took her time joining Alvin. He had thrown the presents carelessly on the sofa and lit up a cigarette. Now, he circled the tree, examining the floor while removing his jacket.

"Where're my gifts?"

"You might still find some buttons in the fireplace," Sadie answered, standing on the golden threshold dividing their living room and the main entrance. "I haven't cleaned the ashes."

Alvin turned to her sharply, dropping his jacket on the floor. "What? The fireplace?"

"I burned them." Sadie stood straight, willing her spine to be as strong as diamonds.

"You're joking. What, did you give away my things to charity again? Come on, I told you to talk to me about that before you go crying over those bums on the street."

"I'm not joking. And I'm now on my way to talk to a lawyer."

"A lawyer?" Alvin took a puff, staring at her as if she had caught him completely off-guard. Maybe she had, what with the way he treated her like a wind-up toy. "For what?"

"A divorce." Sadie gripped her purse. "I hope you'll make this easy. It'll be the best for both of us."

He rolled his eyes. "Christ, woman, you're on *this* again? What's going on? Are you that mad I wasn't here for Christmas? I told you, I had a business meeting. I'm here now, aren't I? We can spend the whole day together."

"And I told you I want a divorce." Sadie kept her gaze pointed directly at him. "I'm also quitting the show. You can take every penny from me, but I'm not going to be your dizzy secretary or your wife anymore."

"Oh, you think you have money?" Alvin bust into laughter and flicked his cigarette into the dark fireplace. "Did you forget *I* bought you all those pretty clothes you're wearing? That all the money you 'earn' is because I was nice enough to give you a spot on *my* successful radio program?"

No, she hadn't forgotten. She knew how difficult this divorce would be. Not only would she have to figure out how to prove he had been mentally cruel to her, but she'd have to find work on her own. She could sell her possessions to get by for a while, but how much could she sell before Alvin locked her out of the house?

In her purse, she had the best of her jewelry and every bit of cash she could scrounge up, just in case she couldn't get back in the house.

"Come on, don't be ridiculous." Alvin stomped toward her. "Whatever you're mad about today, we can work through it."

"No!" Sadie took a step backward. "I said I'm done! It's not just today. It's not even just this year. Our whole marriage, you've taken everything away from me. My independence, my dignity, my dreams, my Clara."

Tears blurred her vision. It had been such a long time since she had cried, she hardly knew what was happening to her. Years of resentment and hurt had been packed so tightly inside her, numbing her nerves. No one—especially Alvin— had ever tried to listen to her or understand her.

No one but Clara.

"Clara?" Alvin now stood close enough that Sadie could smell his lover's perfume. It made her want to vomit. "Why the hell are you bringing up Clara? She's been dead for years."

"So have I!" Sadie turned away from Alvin and tried to march to the front door. Alvin grabbed her arm, stopping her. "Let go of me. I want to live. I can't live with you. I can't live like this."

"You can't live with me?" Alvin squeezed her

arm. "Woman, you've got that all wrong. You can't live *without* me. Remember, woman?"

"It's Sadie!" she screamed, jerking away from him. "My name is Sadie!"

No matter what happened today, Sadie would no longer be anyone except Sadie, the woman who was appreciated just the way she was by Clara.

She just had to get out of the apartment, to the building's elevator, then outside. Alvin wouldn't cause a scene in public. Not when there were so many newspaper spies waiting to find something juicy to report.

He grabbed her again before she could reach the front door and yanked her hat off her head. "You think I'm going to let you humiliate me by making me a divorced man? No, you're going to stay here and talk this out with me. Now, why are you talking about Clara all of a sudden?"

Sadie turned around, flashing him a glare. Fine. If she couldn't leave, then she would stay and fight.

But before she could say anything, she saw Clara hovering behind Alvin. Clara's eyes glowed intensely, revealing every furious thought racing through her.

A shiver rolled through Alvin, and a grin curled in Sadie's lips. Her eyes began to dry.

"I told her you sent me away." Clara's voice came through crystal clear as she spoke into Alvin's ear.

Immediately, Alvin let go of Sadie. He slowly looked over his shoulder. The color drained from his face as he took in the figure standing next to him.

"Oh, no, no, no." Alvin darted for the hallway. "What did you do to me, Sadie? What kind of trick is this?"

"It's not a trick," Sadie said. "Clara came back."

"And I'm not leaving this time."

Clara followed Alvin, her bare feet never touching the ground. His escape lasted for four steps before he sank to his knees. He shook nervously as he clung to the wall, tearing at an expensive Arabic tapestry he had imported.

Sadie stayed in the foyer, watching with fascination.

"Are you going to give Sadie what she wants?"

Clara's presence while she asked that question took up so much space. It was a joy to see Alvin look as small as Sadie had felt for years.

Alvin stared at her, mouth agape. In the last minute, he had aged twenty years.

Clara grew larger. Every part of her shined. The rest of the house seemed so dull, so dark. Sadie's heart raced with excitement.

"If you don't give her what she wants, I'll give it to her," Clara vowed.

She reached for Alvin. He dodged her by rolling away and taking off as quick as his feet would let him move, but Clara had no problem chasing him. They ran into the living room, and then there was a large thud.

Sadie quickly peered into the living room. Alvin lied on the floor, face down, still. Stiller than she had ever seen him. Clara hovered near him, shaking her head.

It seemed the wrath had left Clara's body as she had gone back to her normal size. Her radiance had also dwindled, but it didn't make her any less attractive. There was a distinct peace about her.

"You're free," was all Clara said.

All of this should have been upsetting, but the truth was Sadie just felt relieved.

"Thank you, Clara, darling."

Sadie crossed the living room, delicately stepping over her dead husband, and embraced Clara.

EPILOGUE

MAY 11, 1936

SADIE COULDN'T JUMP INTO HER NEW LIFE RIGHT away. She had to play the part of grieving widow for Alvin's family, friends, coworkers, and the public at large. His death was talked about in the newspapers for about a week. A heart attack, the coroner had ruled, caused by an infection in his body. Sadie weeped before reporters, wishing that Alvin had gone to a hospital instead of a business trip while sick.

"He loved his radio program and wanted to present the best show possible every week," she was quoted in the newspapers. "It was his love for his audience that kept him from thinking of his health first."

After the new year rang in, Alvin's weekly program had been replaced. Another comedian filled the spot. Someone that made everyone forget Alvin B. Reynolds ever existed.

Sadie declined a part on the new show when offered. She had no desire to act, dance, or take part in the entertainment business at all. At thirty-seven, she had retired from her first career. She promised everyone her second career would be something that would make Alvin rest well in the afterlife.

No one had to know she was doing everything possible to make him roll in his grave.

Per Alvin's will, everything had been left to Sadie, provided she didn't remarry within the next three years. Sadie bided her time. Once she had secured his estate, she began chopping everything up. She gave her in-laws half of his money, a token to ensure they wouldn't challenge her for control of the estate. The other half, she donated to various charities in his name, and she made sure every New York newspaper knew about each donation. Alvin's clothes and items, she gave away to people in need. She either donated or sold off the bulk of her own possessions—save for whatever could fit inside two steam trunks—and then sold the palatial apartment on Fifth Avenue along with the summer home in Vermont.

The money would help her establish her new life. She and Clara had decided to move back to Tennessee, but they wouldn't go to Benton.

Instead, they'd open a dress shop in Nashville. Sadie would run the business, and Clara would make the dresses. Despite having been dead for over a decade, Clara proved she could still deftly wield a pair of scissors while possessing Sadie's body.

Clara and Sadie were always together. The past three years had flown by quickly with so much joy and love in their lives. Every day, Sadie woke up, ready to face the world—and Clara was always with her.

The hardest part about the present as a forty-year-old woman who had given up her wealth was staying quiet while Clara made love to her on the train to Tennessee.

Being together in a sleeping berth again had made Clara most amorous, and Sadie also enjoyed the thrill of fucking like the curious twenty-somethings they had once been. Someone slept above them, so they had to be extra careful.

Clara used her powers to restrain Sadie. There wouldn't be any bumps to alarm their sleeping neighbor while Clara teased Sadie. Oh, what a tease she was! She touched Sadie everywhere at once but not enough to make her climax.

"Darling, please, give me more," Sadie groaned softly. "I can't take this anymore."

"*Shh.*" Clara kissed her sweetly. "Keep quiet."

That cold, exhilarating touch made Sadie long for more. But she couldn't voice it.

I'll get you back for this, Sadie thought. Clara smirked.

Restrained and silenced while her lover turned her into a wet mess, it was torture. Sadie hoped this night would last forever.

And if it didn't, that was all right. She knew had the rest of her life to spend with Clara—and the entirety of their afterlives when the time came.

Nothing would separate them ever again.

ABOUT THE AUTHOR

Chace Verity (they/them) is publishing queer as heck stories about romance, friendship, and found families. Chace has published stories in multiple genres including fantasy, paranormal, contemporary, and historical fiction, and it's likely they will keep writing whatever they want. An American citizen and Canadian permanent resident, Chace still isn't sure what a house hippo is.

To receive the latest writing news (and possibly cat photos or horrific doodles) from Chace Verity directly to your inbox, subscribe to their newsletter at chaceverity.com!